Pioneer Christmas Crafts

Heather Patterson

&

Joanna Rice

Photography by Wally Randall

Illustrations by Susan Gardos

SCHOLASTIC CANADA LTD.

In honour of the creativity of our pioneering ancestors,
who brought Christmas cheer to their homes
in a new land

Scholastic Canada Ltd.
175 Hillmount Road, Markham, Ontario L6C 1Z7

Scholastic Inc.
555 Broadway, New York, NY 10012, USA

Scholastic Australia Pty Limited
PO Box 579, Gosford, NSW 2250, Australia

Scholastic New Zealand Limited
Private Bag 94407, Greenmount, Auckland, New Zealand

Scholastic Publications Ltd.
Villiers House, Clarendon Avenue, Leamington Spa,
Warwickshire CV32 5PR, UK

Canadian Cataloguing in Publication Data

Patterson, Heather, 1945–
Pioneer Christmas crafts

ISBN 0-590-51514-4

1. Christmas decorations — Juvenile literature. 2. Handicraft — Juvenile
literature. 3. Frontier and pioneer life — Juvenile literature. I. Rice, Joanna
II. Title.

TT900.C4P37 1999	j745.594'12	C99-930730-4

7 6 5 4 3 2 1   Printed in Canada   9/9 0 1 2 3/0

Introduction

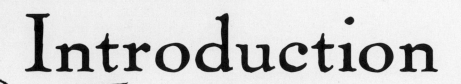

If you had lived in Canada in the 1800s, your home might have been a sod house on the prairie, a log cabin in the woods, a farmhouse on a hill or a brick house in town. But no matter where you lived, Christmas would have been a time for celebration. For Canadian pioneers, Christmas was an occasion for welcoming guests into the home and for enjoying a festive meal with family and friends.

Gifts were not a big part of an early Canadian Christmas. It was not yet the custom, as it is today, to expect a visit from Santa Claus, or to shop for gifts, wrap them and present them to loved ones. Material goods were expensive and hard to come by, and pioneer children were taught to make do with what they had at hand. But with a little spare time, they could easily turn scrap paper, a worn shirt, a leftover piece of wood or an apple from the root cellar into a small, homemade gift for a family member or friend.

In this book are step-by-step instructions for making fifteen crafts, all inspired by those made by Canadian settlers in the 1800s. Many call for simple materials that could either be found around the pioneer home or purchased at the general store. You can find them in your own home, or at a craft, hardware or department store.

✋ A word about safety:

Some of the projects in this book require adult assistance. Dangerous tools and materials have been marked with a hand symbol. Make sure to ask an adult for help with them.

Festive Crackers

Joyeux Noël! At holiday time, children in New France enjoyed pulling open colourful paper crackers and catching the small candies that spilled out. You can make these colourful crackers as gifts or as decorations for the Christmas dinner table.

You will need:

sheets of coloured tissue paper
empty toilet-paper rolls
scissors
white glue
narrow ribbon
assorted hard candies

• Cut one sheet of tissue paper into two. If you like, cut zigzags into the short sides of each sheet.

• Centre a cardboard roll lengthwise at a long side of a sheet. Dot it lightly with glue and attach it to the tissue.

• Roll up the cardboard tube in the sheet, and glue down the seam.

• Cut two equal lengths of ribbon, and use one to tie a tight bow at one end of the roll. Now you can fill your cracker with candies. Just drop a handful into the tube. Tie the other end closed with another ribbon bow.

• Flare the ends of the crackers with your fingers. *Voilà!*

Braided Mat

From the rag bag in every pioneer home came scraps of cloth that were re-used for many purposes, including rag rugs. You can make your own braided mats from old T-shirts! Make them in different sizes to use as a coaster for a teapot or a coffee mug, or to decorate a dollhouse.

You will need:

three old T-shirts (one light-coloured, one medium and one dark)
scissors
a needle and thread
two large safety pins

• Begin by cutting off and discarding the bottom hem of each T-shirt. Then cut across each shirt, making 2.5-cm-wide rings from the bottom up. Snip each ring to make a long strip.

• Gather one strip of each colour and sew them together at one end. Then attach this end to something sturdy, like an armchair, with a safety pin. (Or ask a friend to hold the end for you.)

• Start braiding, keeping the braid as straight and as flat as possible.

• When you have braided almost to the end, secure the braid with another safety pin and sew on three new strips. Continue braiding.

• When you have a long enough braid for your project, fasten the end with a safety pin again.

• Now you're ready to sew the braid into a coil. Thread the needle and knot one end. Working on a table or similar surface, lay the braid flat. Hold the start of the braid with one hand and begin to wind the rest around it. Sew a couple of stitches where the edges meet to hold this in place. Continue winding and sewing, keeping the braid as flat as possible, until you have a finished coil shape.

• Remove the safety pin. Fold the loose end of the braid under and sew it down neatly to the outside edge of the mat.

Bandbox

These small boxes were made to store the lined neckbands worn by gentlemen. Newspaper was used to line them and they were covered with wallpaper. Today's wallpaper is too thick to do the job, but you can cover your box with any other kind of decorative paper. Use it for storing jewellery or other little treasures.

You will need:

a wide-mouthed drinking glass
Bristol board or lightweight cardboard
scissors
a pencil
masking tape
a ruler
wrapping paper or other decorative paper
newspaper
white glue

• Use the drinking glass to draw a circle on the cardboard. This will be the bottom of the box. Cut out the circle and use it to trace another, slighter larger circle onto cardboard. This will be the box lid.

• Cut a rectangle of cardboard large enough to make a tube that will fit upright over the box bottom, allowing for some overlap at the seam. (Use the glass as a guide.) Tape the overlap with masking tape to secure it.

• Use tape to attach the tube to the bottom of the box.

• Cut a 2-cm-wide strip of cardboard, long enough to form the edge of the lid. Make a ring and tape it onto the box lid as you did with the first tube. Check to make sure that the finished lid fits nicely on the box.

• Now your box is ready to cover. Cut a piece of wrapping paper about 2 cm wider and longer than the box tube. Spread the back with a thin layer of glue and wrap it around the tube, leaving about 1 cm of overlap at the top and bottom. With scissors, make 20–30 snips all around each overlap. Fold down the overlap pieces, gluing them in place to the inside edge and bottom of the box.

• Use the box bottom to trace a circle onto the wrapping paper. Cut it out, spread the back with glue, and press it firmly onto the box bottom. Let dry.

• Now cover the box lid in the same way.

• To finish, line the box with newspaper. (This will strengthen it and hide any uneven

edges.) Use the drinking glass to trace two circles of newspaper. Cut these out and glue them firmly to the inside of the lid and the inside bottom of the box. Glue a long, 2-cm-wide strip of newspaper to the inside edge of the lid. Cut wider strips to line the box itself, gluing them in rings around the inside, from bottom to top.

• Let everything dry overnight.

Pomander Ball

Lemons, oranges and apples studded with cloves brought sunny colours and sweet, spicy scents into pioneer homes at Christmastime — and made a welcome gift. Hung with ribbon, they were used to freshen closets or brighten holiday greenery.

You will need:

- **an apple, orange or lemon**
- **a felt marker**
- **whole cloves**
- **a toothpick**
- **scissors**
- **narrow ribbon**

• With the felt marker, draw lines around the fruit to divide the surface into quarters. These lines will be the guides for ribbon that will be added later.

• Push whole cloves into the surface of the fruit. If the fruit you're using has a tough skin, you might need to pierce it with a toothpick first. You can cover the entire fruit (except the ribbon guides), or create any pattern you like. The more cloves you use, the longer your pomander ball will last.

• Let dry overnight.

• Cut two pieces of ribbon about 55 cm long. Wrap the first ribbon around the first guide line and tie it snugly — but don't knot it — at the top. Wrap the second ribbon around the second guide line, and knot this one on top, over the first ribbon. Now take the ends of the first ribbon and tie a bow over the knot.

• Finally, knot together the ends of the second ribbon to form a loop. Now you can hang the pomander ball. (Because the fruit shrinks as it dries, you may need to tighten the ribbon after a few days.)

Log Cabin Block

Many, many winter evenings were devoted to piecing together fabric "blocks" to make beautiful, warm quilts. If you have a few cotton scraps lying around your house, you can make a log cabin quilt block to give as a potholder, wall hanging or doll's blanket. For sewing help, see page 30.

You will need:

cotton fabric in five different shades: red, light, medium-light, medium-dark, dark

a needle and thread

scissors

a ruler

✋ **an iron**

flannelette or quilt batting

ribbon (optional)

twigs (optional)

• Begin with the red fabric. Carefully measure an 8-cm square and cut it out.

• Measure and cut a 4.5-cm-wide strip of each of the other fabrics. The light one (L) should be at least 20.5 cm long, the medium-dark (MD) at least 29.5 cm, the medium-light (ML) at least 38.5 cm, and the dark (D) at least 47.5 cm.

• Line up the edges of the L strip and the red square, good sides together, and pin in place.

• Thread the needle and knot one end. Carefully sew the two pieces together (use the running stitch), 8 mm from the edge, the length of the red square. Sew two or three stitches on top of the last stitch to secure it.

• Press the seam with an iron, making sure that the seam allowances are pressed away from the red centre.

• Cut off the rest of the L strip. Now, with the partly sewn block good side up, and the strip you just added at the top, pin the remaining piece of the L strip *to the right side*. Stitch together in the same way. Press, and cut off any excess.

• Attach the MD strip to the third and fourth sides of the red square in the same way: pin, sew, press, cut and repeat. You now have a square.

• Rotating around the red centre in the same direction, add the ML strip on the next two sides, and finish up with the D strip on the last two sides. You have made a log cabin block.

• To make a small mat or doll's quilt, cut a piece of fabric the same size as your square for the quilt backing. Line up the edges of the backing and the block, good sides together, and pin. Sew in a running stitch around three sides, 8 mm from the edge. Turn the mat right-side out and gently press it with an iron.

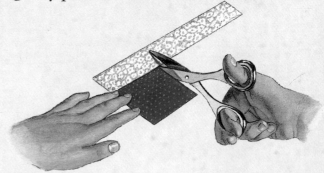

• Cut a slightly smaller piece of flannelette or quilt batting. Slip it in between the block and the backing, fitting it into the corners and pinning it in place. Then fold under the open edges 8 mm and overcast-stitch them together.

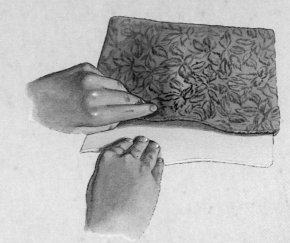

• With pencil and ruler, lightly draw an X on the front, from corner to corner. Sew in a running stitch to quilt the three layers together.

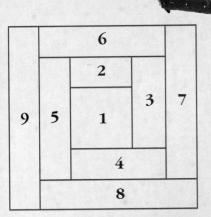

• To make a wall hanging, pin and stitch in place two ribbon loops as you sew up the last side. Then slip a twig through the loops.

Red has always been used for the centre of a traditional log cabin block. It represents the glowing fire in the hearth. The darker half of the block represents shade and the lighter half, sunshine.

Pretty Paper

Stencilled Stationery

Stencilling was a technique used to decorate the walls, floors and furniture of pioneer homes. Use it to make a pretty sheaf of stencilled paper for letter writing!

You will need:

a pencil or pen

Bristol board or a disposable plastic container lid

newspaper

✋ a utility knife

sheets of writing paper

craft paints and sponge

ribbon

• Plan your stencil design on paper. Keep to one or two simple shapes for easiest cutting. Draw the shapes onto Bristol board or a plastic container lid.

• Spread a thick layer of newspaper over your cutting surface. Use the utility knife to carefully cut out the stencil design.

• Position the stencil on a sheet of writing paper where you'd like the design to appear. Dip the sponge into the paint and blot it on a scrap piece of paper to remove any excess — the drier, the better! Then sponge the paint over the stencil.

• Let dry, and repeat the pattern if you like.

• Tie the finished sheets neatly together with fancy ribbon.

Autograph Album

Albums were popular in early times for recording lines of poetry and collecting autographs. You can make one by binding sheets of paper between decorated covers with a pretty ribbon.

You will need:

a pencil and ruler

Bristol board or cardboard

scissors

a hole punch

✋ a utility knife

sheets of paper

felt markers or craft paints and brush

glue (optional)

ribbon

• Using a ruler, draw a rectangle onto a scrap of Bristol board or cardboard, and cut it out for the front cover. Punch at least two holes along one side. Cut out a second rectangle the same size, and punch holes in the same spots, using the front cover as a guide.

• Now score the outside of the front cover: with the utility knife, lightly cut a line about 1 cm in from the holes (and parallel to them) so that the cover will open easily. (Don't cut right through the cover.)

• Cut as many inside pages as you like from scrap paper. They can be the same size as the covers or slightly smaller. Stack the pages, making sure they are all lined up on the left side. Then, using the cover as a guide, punch holes through all the sheets.

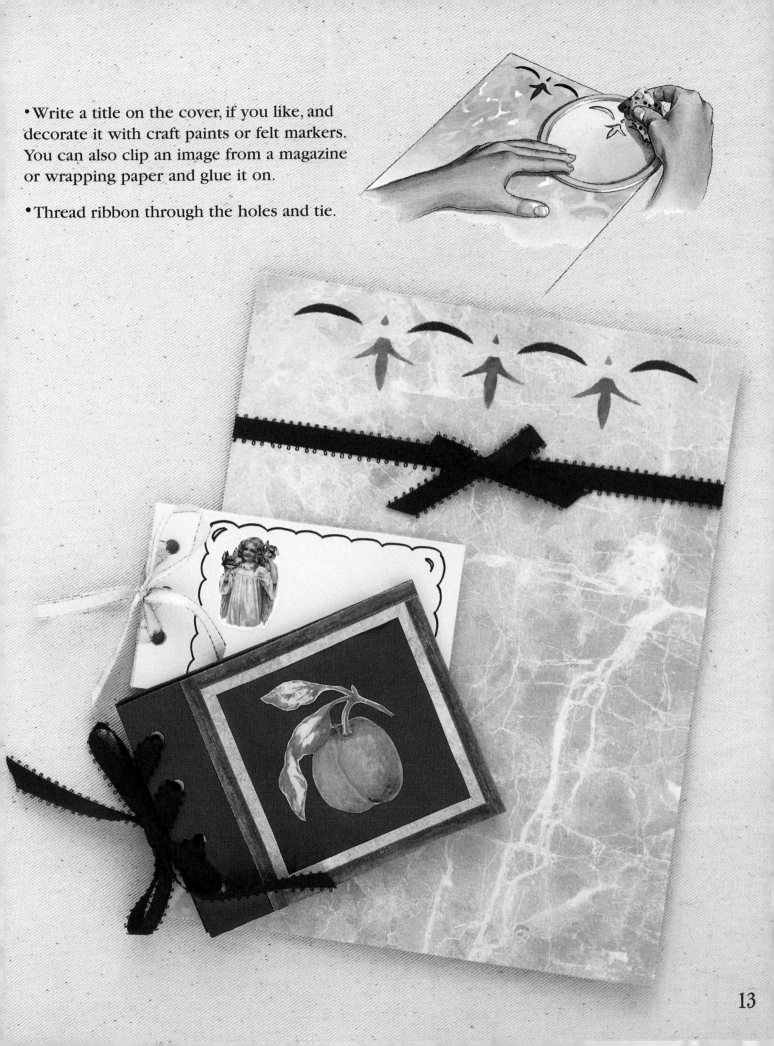

• Write a title on the cover, if you like, and decorate it with craft paints or felt markers. You can also clip an image from a magazine or wrapping paper and glue it on.

• Thread ribbon through the holes and tie.

Checkerboard

Checkers was a favourite game in pioneer times. Boards were usually homemade, and the playing pieces were sometimes humble corncob slices! This checkerboard will look especially nice hung on a wall when not in use.

You will need:

sheet of 1/4" plywood or masonite, cut to 37 cm x 52 cm

4 pieces of 3/4" x 1/2" wood trim: 2 at 33 cm long and 2 at 52 cm long

sandpaper

a pencil and ruler

carpenter's glue

newspaper

craft paints in red and black

2 paintbrushes (one straight-edged)

a set of checkers

✋ **polyurethane (optional)**

• Lightly sand edges of all wood pieces until smooth.

• Use the pencil and ruler to draw a border along all four sides of the board, 2 cm in from the edge. Draw two more lines, one along each of the short sides, 7.5 cm in from the border. Now you have a 33-cm-square playing surface in the centre of the board.

• With the pencil and ruler, divide the playing surface into four quarters, each 16.5 cm square. Divide each quarter in four, so you have 16 equal 8.25-cm squares. Finally, divide all 16 squares into quarters again. You should end up with 64 perfect 4.125-cm squares!

• Using carpenter's glue, attach the two 52-cm pieces of trim to the long sides of the board. Then glue the shorter pieces of trim to the short sides. Press firmly, and let dry overnight. You may want to clamp these while they dry.

• Spread a thick layer of newspaper over your work surface. Now it's time to paint the checkerboard. To make this as easy as possible, paint the entire 33-cm-square area with the red craft paint. Let dry. Re-mark the lines, if necessary, to make them more visible through the paint.

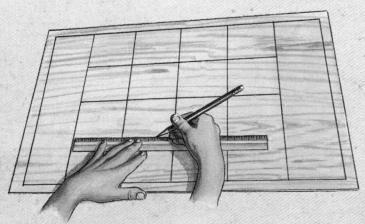

• Using the straight-edged brush, very carefully fill in every other square with black paint. Take your time.

• Now paint the ends. When these are dry, add a design, if you like, to make your board unique.

• Paint the trim, and let dry.

• Finish with a coat of polyurethane, if you like.

Most lumber centres will cut your wood to measure before you buy it.

Cookie Ornaments

Sweet treats have always been a special part of Christmas. In German pioneer homes, *lebkuchen* (gently spiced "life cakes") were cut into festive shapes, baked and hung on the tree. The dough should be made a day ahead of time and allowed to chill.

You will need:

350 mL sifted flour
5 mL ground cinnamon
2 mL ground cloves
1 mL ground nutmeg
pinch of salt
90 mL honey
30 mL light molasses
75 mL brown sugar
15 mL orange juice
1 egg
60 mL candied fruit, chopped
1 mL baking soda
5 mL hot water
125 mL slivered almonds, finely chopped
cookie cutters (optional)

• In a medium-sized bowl, sift flour, spices and salt together. Set aside.

• In a large bowl, mix honey and molasses, add brown sugar, and mix well. Stir in orange juice.

• Beat the egg in a small bowl, and add about a third of it to the sugar mixture. (Save the rest for brushing over the cookie tops before baking.)

• Dust candied fruit with flour; add to sugar mixture. Then mix hot water with baking soda and add this to the mixture as well.

• Gradually add the flour mixture to the sugar mixture, stirring to blend. Add chopped almonds. Stir into a stiff dough.

• Form the dough into a ball, and store it in a plastic bag in the fridge overnight.

• The next day, roll out the dough to a 5-mm thickness, and cut out shapes with cookie cutters or a knife. Pierce a hole in the top of each one.

• Mix the remainder of the beaten egg with 5 mL water, and brush it over the cookie tops.

✋ Bake on a greased cookie sheet for 12–15 minutes at 175°C (350°F).

These cookies are edible, but very hard and chewy. Thread them with ribbon to make perfect tree ornaments!

This recipe makes about two dozen cookies.

> Once cooled, cookie ornaments can be decorated with "royal icing" — a stiff blend of icing sugar and egg whites.

Beaded Needle Case

A little needle case was a useful way to store needles and pins. Do you know someone who might need to sew on a button, or mend a torn seam? This pretty felt case, decorated with beads, will bring a smile to the task!

You will need:

felt
tracing paper (optional)
a pencil and a felt marker
scissors
a very fine needle, and thread
beads
a variety of needles and pins

• Use tracing paper to trace the pattern on this page (or make your own pattern) and cut it out. Trace around it on a piece of felt, and cut out. Repeat until you have five layers altogether. (You can use different colours if you like.) Pin the layers together, along the straight edge, to hold them firmly in place.

• Thread a needle — with a matching colour thread, if possible — and knot the ends of the thread together. Starting from the back side, make small and even running stitches along the straight edge through all five layers of felt. Finish by tying a knot at the back.

• Now you can decorate the cover of your needle case with beads. With the felt marker, draw a simple guide line on the top layer — follow the scalloped edge, or create your own design. Next, choose the bead colour or colours you will use.

• Thread a needle and knot the ends of the thread together. Starting on the back side of the *top layer* (don't sew through to the other layers!), push the needle through to the top, and string three beads onto the needle. Push them all the way down the thread until they are sitting on your guide line, and sew through to the back side again, as close as possible to the last bead. Bring the needle through to the top again, add three beads, and so on. If your design has any sharp turns in it, you may have to add fewer beads at a time in those places. When you're done, tie a knot at the back.

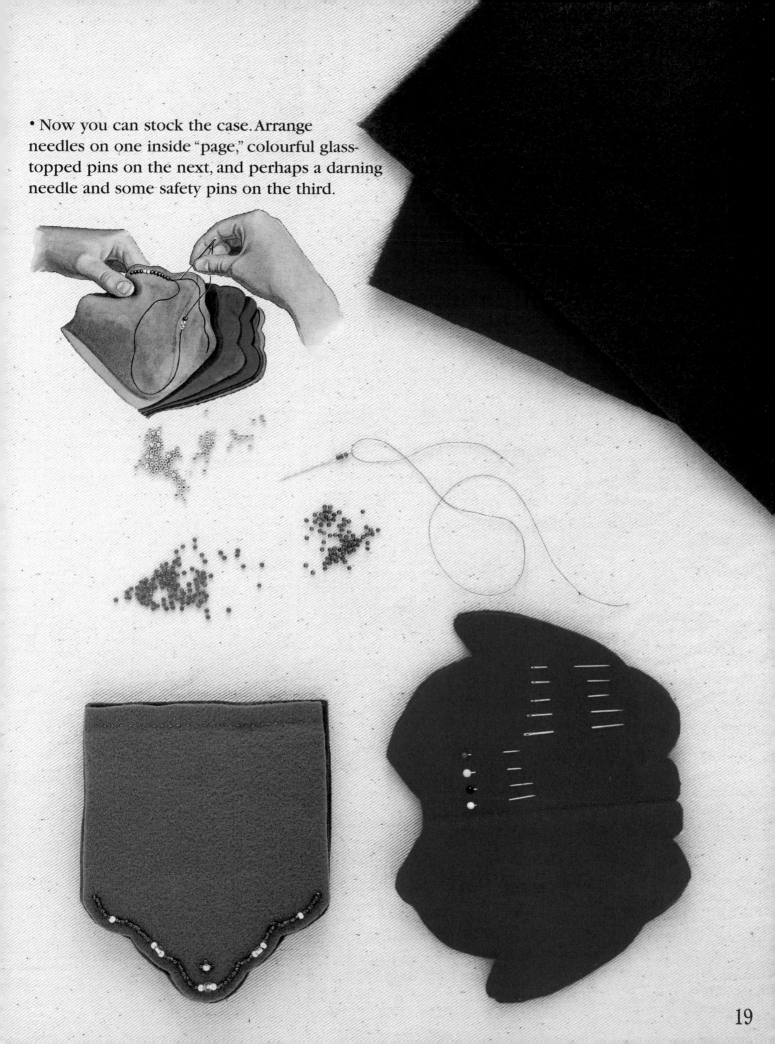

• Now you can stock the case. Arrange needles on one inside "page," colourful glass-topped pins on the next, and perhaps a darning needle and some safety pins on the third.

19

Painted Glass

Glass bottles, jars and small vases painted with pretty designs made an attractive gift in pioneer times. You too can decorate glass to give to a friend!

You will need:

a small glass container
a pencil and paper
newspaper
craft paints and fine brush
clear nail polish
ribbon
dried flowers or cinnamon sticks (optional)

• Plan a design for your glass container on paper.

• Spread a thick layer of newspaper over your work surface.

• Paint directly on the glass, following your design. Start with one colour and let dry before continuing with the next.

• When you have finished and the paint is completely dry, brush clear nail polish over the design to protect it.

• When the polish is dry, finish by tying on a pretty ribbon, if you like. You can also slip in a few cinnamon sticks, or a sprig of dried flowers.

21

Cross-Stitch Picture

If you had lived one hundred and fifty years ago, you probably would have learned to cross-stitch at an early age. A gingham background makes it easy!

You will need:

cotton gingham fabric
graph paper (optional)
a pencil and ruler
a large-eyed needle; embroidery floss
✋ **an iron**
scissors
corrugated cardboard
thin cardboard
white glue
newspaper
✋ **an awl and hammer**
narrow ribbon
twigs
✋ **pruning shears (optional)**

• Decide on the size of the finished "picture" you would like to make, and choose a piece of gingham about 4 cm longer and wider. Work out where the letters for your message will appear on the fabric, using the squares to plan the spacing. Use graph paper, if you like.

• Choose a contrasting colour of embroidery floss and separate the six strands into threes. Thread three strands onto the needle, and knot at one end.

• Begin cross-stitching your picture. For instructions, see page 30. Whenever the thread runs out, just tie a single knot at the back, re-thread the needle and continue where you left off.

• Press your finished work with an iron.

• Cut a piece of corrugated cardboard to the size of your finished picture, and centre the cross-stitch design over it. Wrap the excess fabric around to the back and glue it down. Then cut a piece of thin cardboard, about 1 cm smaller all around than the thicker piece, and glue it on the back to cover the raw fabric edges.

• Now make the ribbon holes. Mark them first on the back: there should be two holes at each of the four corners, and they should be about 2 cm apart — see photo, opposite.

• Spread a thick layer of newspaper over your work surface. Use an awl and hammer to punch holes right through the cardboard and fabric to the front of the picture.

• Cut four 30-cm-long pieces of ribbon. Using the needle, thread ribbon through one hole, from the front to the back. Then thread it through the adjacent hole and pull it back up to the front. Adjust the ribbons so the ends are of equal length.

• Choose four twigs: two about 2 cm longer than the long sides of the picture, and two about 2 cm longer than the short sides (or use pruning shears to trim twigs to fit). Lay the side pieces in place. Then lay the top and bottom twigs over them. Now tie each ribbon into a snug bow over the crossed twigs at the corners.

Birchbark Box

The native people of eastern Canada made waterproof birchbark containers for collecting sap from maple trees. They used one or two stitches of split spruce root to fasten the box. You can make a small birchbark box, tied with yarn and filled with nuts.

You will need:

birchbark from a fallen log or dead tree

a pencil and ruler

scissors

newspaper

clothespins or paper clips

a large-eyed needle and yarn or embroidery floss

unshelled nuts

• Soak a wide strip of birchbark in water overnight. Weigh it down with a brick or a heavy rock.

• Lay the wet bark on a thick layer of newspaper. Cut a 20-cm square from the best part of the bark. Now peel off the first few layers from the white side. This side will become the inside of the container. To make the bark easier to bend without snapping, you may need to peel a few layers off the brown side, as well. If necessary, spray the bark with water to keep it moist.

• With a pencil, draw an enlarged version of the pattern shown at right onto the lighter side. The centre square will be the bottom of the container. Cut around the pattern.

• Crease all solid lines. Bring points A and B together by folding along the dotted diagonal line. Fold the point against the square beside it, and clip to hold. Repeat at the other three corners.

• Using the darning needle, make four holes at each folded side, as shown opposite. Then thread the needle with red yarn or embroidery floss. Criss-cross it through the holes on one side, and tie on the inside with a double knot. Repeat on the other side.

• Fill the finished box with nuts.

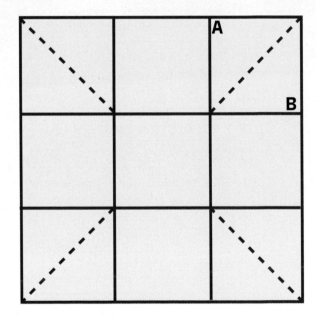

NEVER peel bark from living birch trees! It will cause them to weaken and die. If you cannot find any bark from a fallen log or dead tree, you can draw a birchbark design on Bristol board instead.

Monogrammed Napkin

Embroidering initials on one's belongings was an attractive way to mark them as one's own. You can embroider a cloth napkin with a friend's initial. It can be tucked into a lunchbox or used at the table.

You will need:

loose-woven fabric scrap and scissors (or a ready-made cloth napkin)

a pencil

a large-eyed needle and embroidery floss

✋ an iron

• Cut a 40-cm square of fabric (or use a ready-made cloth napkin). To fray the edges of the napkin, pull out the threads running parallel to the edge until the frayed edge is about 2 cm wide.

• Use the pencil to draw a plain or fancy initial at one corner.

• Choose a contrasting colour of embroidery floss and separate the six strands into threes. Thread three strands onto a needle, and knot one end.

• Stem-stitch along the pencil lines. (See diagram below.) Knot on the back of the napkin whenever the thread runs out. Try to make small, even stitches. Check the back of your work regularly to make sure that the thread is being pulled through completely.

• Press your work with an iron when you're done.

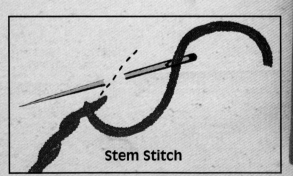

Stem Stitch

Jolly Jumping Jack

Children of pioneer times had few toys, but a jumping jack was a simple toy they could easily make themselves. You can make one to hang on the Christmas tree or to decorate a present. Hold onto the hat and pull the hanging string. Your jack will jump!

You will need:

tracing paper (optional)
Bristol board or thin cardboard
a pencil
scissors
brass paper-fasteners
string
felt markers, coloured pencils or craft paints and brush
ribbon

• Either trace the pattern on this page and transfer it to Bristol board or cardboard, or use the pattern as a guide for drawing directly onto cardboard.

• Mark the joints (black dots) and string holes (blue dots) on the cardboard and cut out all pieces. Start holes for the joints with a toothpick or pencil, then rotate a paper fastener in the holes until they widen. Make slightly smaller holes for the string.

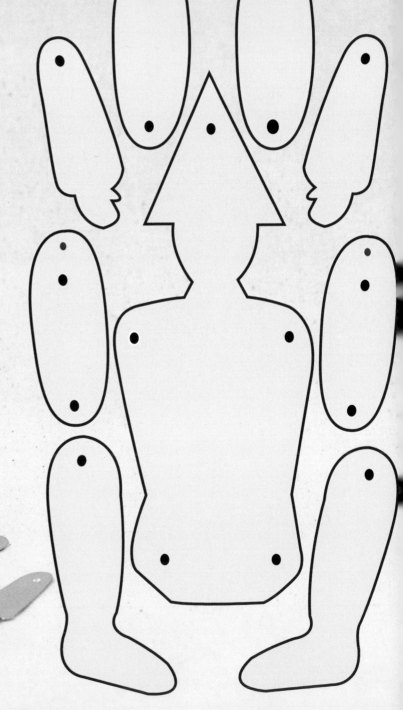

• Paint your jumping jack. Let all pieces dry.

• Attach the limbs to the body with brass fasteners, as shown below. If the fasteners are large, hide them by folding the tabs back on themselves.

• String your jumping jack with three separate pieces of string: two 10 cm long and one 30 cm long. Thread one end of a 10-cm string through one shoulder hole, loop and knot firmly. Then thread the other end through the opposite shoulder hole, loop, knot, and trim away any excess. Tie the hips in the same way with the other 10-cm string. Finally, knot one end of the long string at the mid-point of the shoulder string, knot it again at the mid-point of the hip string, and let the rest hang down below.

• Finish by tying a loop of ribbon through the jumping jack's hat.

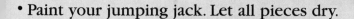

Sewing Tips

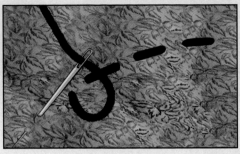

Running Stitch

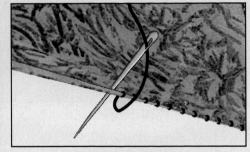

Overcast Stitch

- For easiest sewing, the distance from the needle to the knot should be no longer than your arm.

- Seam allowance: the area between the seam and the fabric edge.

How to Cross-Stitch

Cross-stitching is simply making a series of Xs in rows. There are two basic ways to do this.

For single cross-stitches, push your needle through to the front of the fabric at the bottom left corner of a square and push it back down at the top right. Bring it out again at the bottom right and back down at the top left. For the next stitch, move one square to the right or left and repeat.

In the second method, the Xs are completed in two journeys. Make a series of diagonal stitches across an entire row, then work back to the beginning of the row, completing the Xs. Bring the needle through to the front of the fabric at the bottom left corner of the first square, then push it back down at the top right. Move to the next square and repeat, continuing until you reach the end of the row. When you get there, bring the needle back through to the front at the bottom right corner of the last square, and repeat stitches in the opposite direction. (Note: for the Cross-Stitch Picture project, four squares were used for each cross-stitch.)

It's up to you to use the method you prefer. The only rule that applies to both is this: make sure that the first halves of the Xs all slope in the same direction.

If you make mistakes at first, just pick out the stitches and redo them. Soon the pattern will make sense, and you'll be surprised to find that your fingers remember what to do!

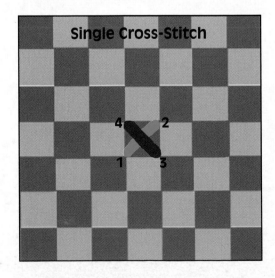

Single Cross-Stitch

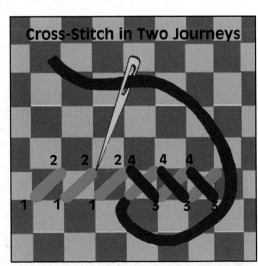

Cross-Stitch in Two Journeys

LOVELY, LOVELY PIRATE GOLD

First published 2007
Evans Brothers Limited
2A Portman Mansions
Chiltern St
London W1U 6NR

British Library Cataloguing in Publication Data

Anderson, Scoular
    Lovely lovely pirate gold. - (Zig zag)
    1. Pirates - Juvenile fiction 2. Treasure troves - Juvenile
    fiction 3. Maps - Juvenile fiction 4. Children's stories
    I. Title
    823.9'14[J]

ISBN-10: 0 237 53166 6 (hb)
13 digit ISBN: 978 0237 53166 9
ISBN-10: 0 237 53170 4 (pb)
13 digit ISBN: 978 0237 53170 6

Printed in China

Series Editor: Nick Turpin
Design: Robert Walster
Production: Jenny Mulvanny

LOVELY, LOVELY PIRATE GOLD

by Scoular Anderson

Evans

When the pirate captain
opened his chest…

…looking for socks and
an itchy vest…

...he found – a map!

He ran to his crew...

"You know what to do
with this wonderful clue –
it's time to hunt for treasure."

So they sailed away...

...to a wide, sandy bay...

13

...where they all
lent a hand...

...to dig in the sand.

15

The sand piled up as they dug for loot…

...but they found no treasure,
just a smelly old boot!

19

The captain cried, "It's just not fair!"
Then stamped his foot and pulled his hair.

The cabin boy looked at the map...

...first like this, then like that.

23

At last he told them with
a frown,
"The treasure map was
upside down!"

24

They raced away to
dig again.

This time the captain did not complain!

Then each pirate wore a smile,
when each pirate had a pile
of lovely, lovely pirate gold.

30

31

Why not try reading another ZigZag book?

Dinosaur Planet ISBN 0 237 52667 0
by David Orme and Fabiano Fiorin

Tall Tilly ISBN 0 237 52668 9
by Jillian Powell and Tim Archbold

Batty Betty's Spells ISBN 0 237 52669 7
by Hilary Robinson and Belinda Worsley

The Thirsty Moose ISBN 0 237 52666 2
by David Orme and Mike Gordon

The Clumsy Cow ISBN 0 237 52656 5
by Julia Moffat and Lisa Williams

Open Wide! ISBN 0 237 52657 3
by Julia Moffatt and Anni Axworthy

Too Small ISBN 0 237 52777 4
by Kay Woodward and Deborah van de Leigraaf

I Wish I Was An Alien ISBN 0 237 52776 6
by Vivian French and Lisa Williams

The Disappearing Cheese ISBN 0 237 52775 8
by Paul Harrison and Ruth Rivers

Terry the Flying Turtle ISBN 0 237 52774 X
by Anna Wilson and Mike Gordon

Pet To School Day ISBN 0 237 52773 1
by Hilary Robinson and Tim Archbold

The Cat in the Coat ISBN 0 237 52772 3
by Vivian French and Alison Bartlett

Pig in Love ISBN 0 237 52950 5
by Vivian French and Tim Archbold

The Donkey That Was Too Fast ISBN 0 237 52949 1
by David Orme and Ruth Rivers

The Yellow Balloon ISBN 0 237 52948 3
by Helen Bird and Simona Dimitri

Hamish Finds Himself ISBN 0 237 52947 5
by Jillian Powell and Belinda Worsley

Flying South ISBN 0 237 52946 7
by Alan Durant and Kath Lucas

Croc by the Rock ISBN 0 237 52945 9
by Hilary Robinson and Mike Gordon

Turn off the Telly! ISBN 0 237 53168 2
by Charlie Gardner and Barbara Nascimbeni

Fred and Finn ISBN 0 237 53169 0
by Madeline Goodey and Mike Gordon

A Mouse in the House ISBN 0 237 53167 4
by Vivian French and Tim Archbold

Lovely, Lovely Pirate Gold ISBN 0 237 53170 4
by Scoular Anderson